Swine Divine

by **Jan Carr** illustrated by **Robert Bender**

Holiday House • New York

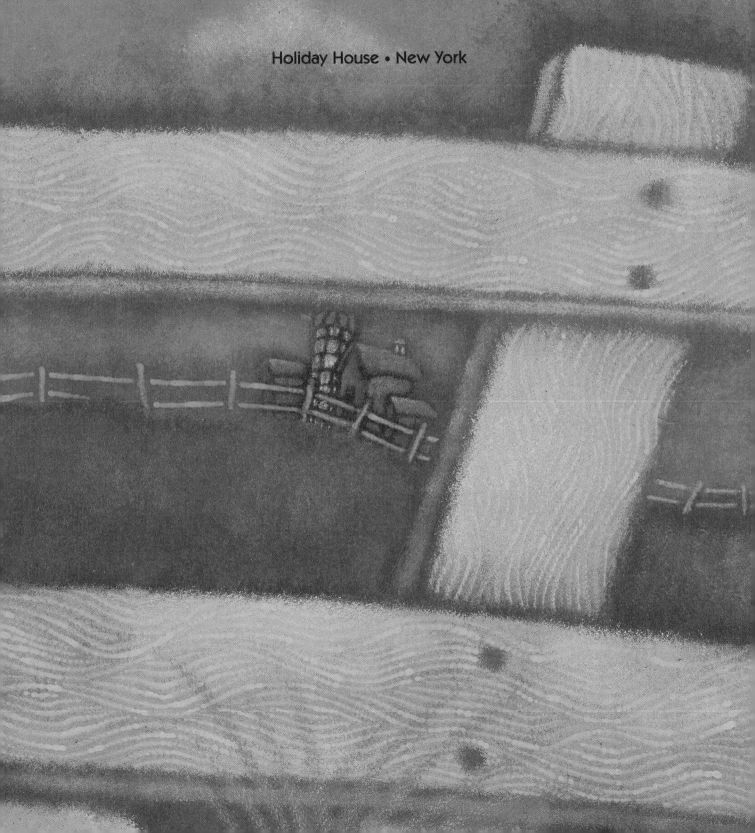

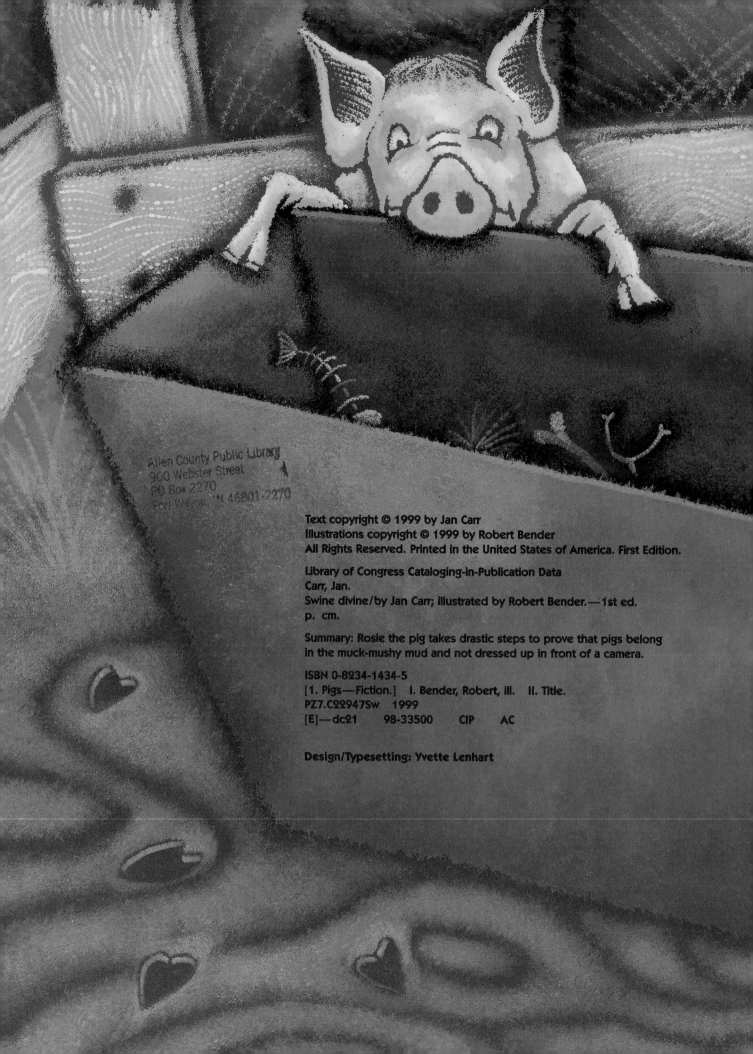

Text copyright © 1999 by Jan Carr
Illustrations copyright © 1999 by Robert Bender
All Rights Reserved. Printed in the United States of America. First Edition.

Library of Congress Cataloging-in-Publication Data
Carr, Jan.
Swine divine/by Jan Carr; illustrated by Robert Bender.—1st ed.
p. cm.

Summary: Rosie the pig takes drastic steps to prove that pigs belong
in the muck-mushy mud and not dressed up in front of a camera.

ISBN 0-8234-1434-5
[1. Pigs—Fiction.]   I. Bender, Robert, ill.   II. Title.
PZ7.C22947Sw   1999
[E]—dc21   98-33500   CIP   AC

Design/Typesetting: Yvette Lenhart

For Stan, who slops the swill,
and Charlie, our little piglet
J. C.

In loving memory of Paula,
Eugene, Kopel, and Sophie
R. B.

It was a pig-perfect morning. As the pale, pearly light broke over the quiet farm, Luke carried a bucket of swill to the sty. He spilled the swill into the big tin trough. Rosie ate her fill.

When she was finished, Rosie wallowed in the sprawl of the big, muddy hollow. Rosie loved to be covered with mud. From the snip of her snout to the tip of her tail.

"That's my Rosie," Luke said proudly.

Flies flew overhead, buzzing a busy, dizzy lullaby. Rosie felt drowsy and dozy. She stretched out into the muck-mushy mud and started to drift back to sleep.

Splash! Rosie awoke with a start. Someone was spraying her with a hose!

"Got to git you scrubbed up," said Luke.

Scrubbed up? What for?

"Mr. Porkpie's awaitin'. I promised him you'd ham it up."

Ham? **"Oink!"** squealed Rosie. The last thing she wanted to be was a ham!

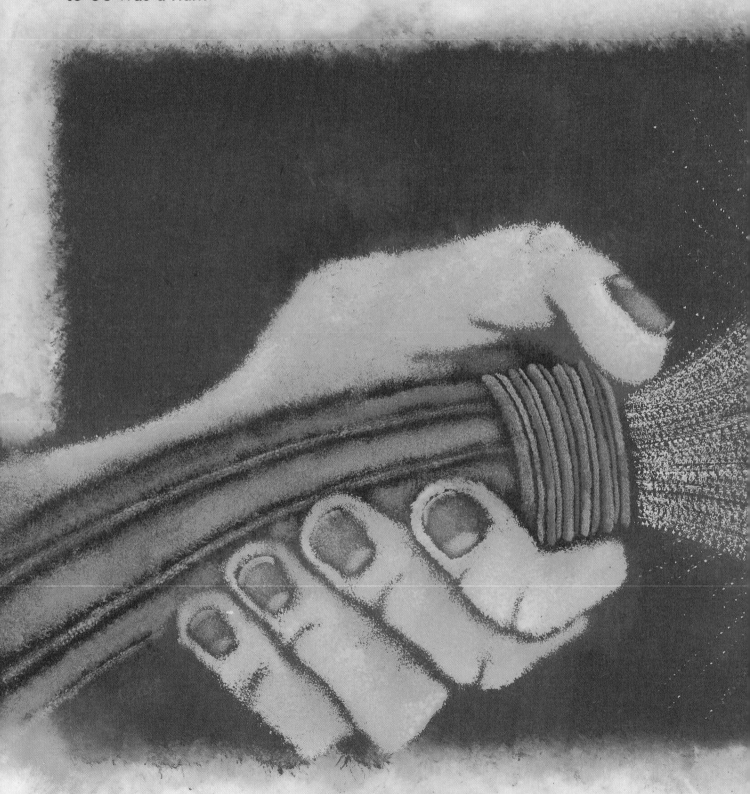

Luke picked up Rosie and put her in her cage. He strapped her to the back of his bicycle, then peddled the long, dirt road that led to town.

Rosie pressed her snout against the hard bars of the cage. Above her, clouds gathered, darkening the sky. A raindrop fell on Rosie's head. **Splish-splash!** More streamed down, streaking Rosie's face like sad, soppy tears. The farm moved farther and farther in the distance.

Luke carried Rosie into a cold, stone store. Strange equipment towered over her, long armed and monstrous. Mr. Porkpie hoisted Rosie high. Her legs dangled down like plump, lumpy sausages.

"Scrumptious!" cried Mr. Porkpie, smacking his lips. "What a pudgy little piglet! Let's shoot her right now!"

Rosie froze.

Mr. Porkpie rooted through some clothes on a rack. He tied a bonnet around Rosie's chin. The bow was tight. She could barely breathe.

Flash! A bright light blinded Rosie. Mr. Porkpie shot her picture.

"Magnificent!" he cried. "I'll call this photograph 'Pig in a Poke.'"

Next, Mr. Porkpie set Rosie in a big pot filled with fuzzy fake flowers. The petals tickled her nose.

Flash! A bright light blinded Rosie. Mr. Porkpie shot her picture.

"Inspired!" he exclaimed. "I'll call this portrait 'Hog in the Hollyhocks.'"

Then Mr. Porkpie fastened something around Rosie's belly, something stiff and starchy. Rosie's skin felt tight and itchy. She felt all pig-wriggly.

"My masterpiece!" declared Mr. Porkpie. "I'll call this shot 'Swine Divine.'"

Swine Divine? For the love of mud, Rosie had had enough! She leaped to the floor and tore across the room.

Bang! Rosie knocked down the camera!

Boom! Rosie toppled the lights!

Bam! She ran through the rack of clothes, scattering the costumes helter-skelter! Rosie was running hog wild!

"Get that pig!" shouted Mr. Porkpie.

Rosie bolted out the door and loped down the street. Luke hopped on his bicycle and chased after her. Pedestrians jumped clear of them. **Honk!** Cars skidded and swerved. Rosie ran and ran.

Finally, Rosie reached the farm. She threw herself whole-hog in the mud. She rolled and rolled with all her soul. Luke came running toward her.

"Rosie!" he shouted. "Why'd you run off like that? You looked right cute in that tutu!"

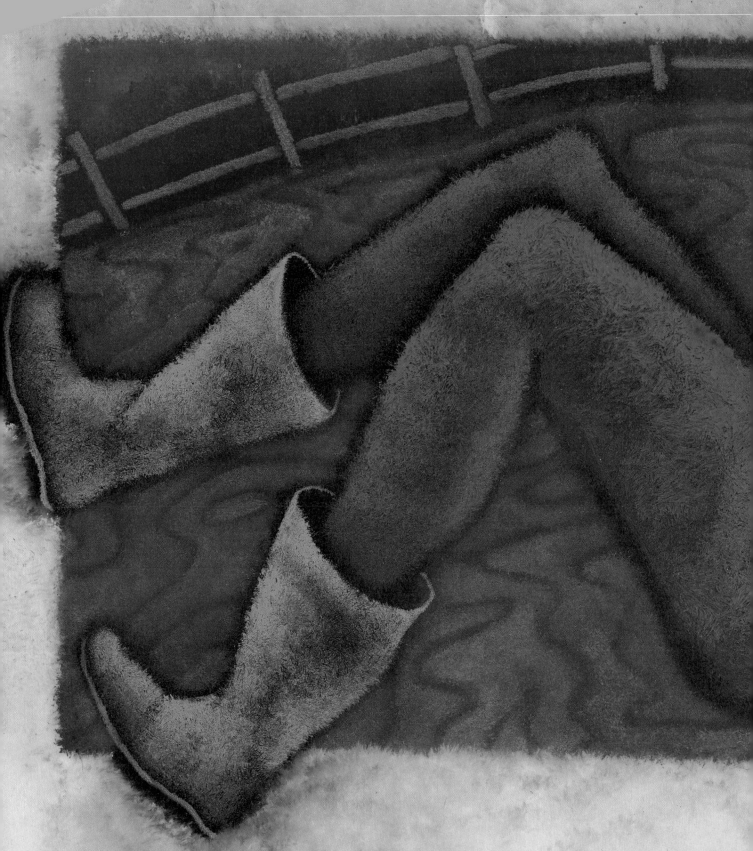

Hogwash! Rosie ran at Luke. **Splat!** Luke fell flat in the mud.

"Oink!" Rosie told him off. **"Oink! Oink!"**

Luke looked at Rosie, who loved to be covered with mud. From the snip of her snout to the tip of her tail. Luke unhooked the tutu. Maybe Rosie had a point. Maybe she did look better without it.

High in the sky, the sun peeped through the clouds, warming the land. Flies flew overhead, buzzing their busy, dizzy lullaby. Rosie sprawled out in the mud and slipped back to sleep.

"Oinnnnkkkkk," she snored loudly.

Swinely. Divinely.

She dreamed of a heaven, Hog Heaven, where mud
stretched as far as a pig's eye could see.